THE CHRISTMAS WITCH

Retold and Illustrated by
ILSE PLUME

WITH BEST WISHES from ILSE PLUME

Hyperion Books for Children

Text and Illustrations Copyright © 1981 by Ilse Plume

All rights reserved.

Printed in the United States of America

FIRST EDITION

10   9   8   7   6   5   4   3   2   1

ISBN: TRADE 1-56282-077-X / ISBN: LIBRARY 1-56282-078-8

This book was previously published
in 1981 by David R. Godine, Publisher, Inc.

Library of Congress Cataloging in Publication Number 91-71380

To the freckle-faced sunshine kid
my daughter Anne-Marie

and to the miracle worker in my life
Jane Langton

with love and gratitude

There are many kind spirits in Italy. One of the nicest is Befana, the Christmas Witch. She is as much a part of the Christmas tradition in Italy as Santa Claus in America.

Like Santa Claus, Befana appears only once a year. She comes twelve days after Christmas during the festival of Epiphany, which celebrates the visit of the three wise men to the infant Jesus. Her name, Befana, is derived from the word *Epifania,* the Italian name for that religious festival.

Long ago, people thought she was an evil old witch. They rang bells of clay and blew glass trumpets to frighten her away. Now they know she is a kind and gentle spirit, and her gifts are awaited eagerly by all the children of Italy.

The miracle of Befana is not in history books, but every Italian child knows that her magic will return every year.

A very long time ago a woman lived in a small house in the Tuscan hills of Italy. Her name was Befana. Because she could tell fortunes and heal the sick, people thought she had magical powers. Although she had no children, Befana had six cats and a bird in a cage. The bird's name was Uccellino, or Little Bird.

Befana's house was on a hill, and at the bottom of the hill was a forest where she could gather sticks for firewood. One day she went down the hill many times. She returned each time with her arms full of sticks, so by sundown she was very tired. But there was still one more bundle of sticks at the bottom of the hill.

'I must get it all,' said Befana, 'or old Giovanni, the woodcutter, will steal it again.'

Then she stopped at her gate in surprise —she could hear bells. Far away there were riders approaching on the road.

They came closer. Three men, mounted on camels, stopped beside Befana's gate. The camels were laden with rich gifts and bags of gold. The men looked old and wise and were dressed in splendid robes.

'We come from a far country,' said one of the Wise Men. 'We are looking for the Christ Child, who is born in Bethlehem. Good woman, can you tell us the way?'

'Bethlehem?' said Befana. 'It is there across the mountains and valleys, beyond the great seas.'

Turning to point the way, she was astonished to see a great star shining in the sky.

'The star!' cried the Wise Man. 'God has sent a splendid shining star to lead us to the child. Perhaps we are nearing the end of our journey. But, good woman, have you not heard of this great miracle?'

Befana's eyes grew wide with wonder. The star shone more brightly than any she had ever seen. Surely these were not ordinary travellers.

'I live by myself,' said Befana. 'I did not know such a baby had been born. Oh, please, may I come with you?'

'Yes, good woman, you may come with us,' said the Wise Man. 'But you must come at once. We cannot stay. We must not lose sight of the star.'

'Oh, Sir,' said Befana, 'please wait until I gather the rest of my firewood. If I go with you now, Giovanni will steal it. And then I will not have enough wood to keep warm.'

But the Wise Man was pointing to the star and beckoning to the others to follow. The camels were moving away.

'And a gift for the baby,' cried Befana. 'I must bring toys for the Christ Child!'

Running down the hill, Befana snatched up the last bundle of sticks and struggled back up again with her heavy burden.

The riders were gone, and a dark cloud had hidden the star.

Befana was alone and forlorn. She had only her cats and Uccellino, her bird, to comfort her. Sadly she crept into bed.

But the next morning, the orange sun rose over the purple mountains and streamed into Befana's bedroom, and Uccellino began to sing. Filled with happiness, Befana jumped out of bed. No longer did she feel tired. The weariness in her bones had vanished overnight. She felt she could float on air.

Humming to herself, Befana dressed, made her breakfast, and fed Uccellino and the six cats. Then she ran next door to ask old Signora Martinelli, the pastamaker, to care for them.

At last she was ready to go. But when she looked around her house to find presents for the Christ Child, she could find nothing to bring to the baby.

Sadly she put on her boots and her old red cape. It was better to go empty-handed than not to go at all.

But when Befana had said goodby to the cats and Uccellino, she found a miracle lying on the floor beside her back door —a large grey sack filled to the brim with toys.

Befana clapped her hands with joy. Then, slinging the heavy sack over her shoulder, she closed the door tightly and went on her way.

And so Befana's long, long journey began.

Searching for the star and the Wise Men, she travelled around the world. Her sack never grew heavy. Befana never grew tired.

But she never caught up with the star. She never saw the Wise Men.

One day just after sunset she came to a farm in a small village. A thousand stars began to twinkle in the sky. Two shepherds were guarding a flock of sheep.

The shepherds were surprised to see a stranger. 'Good woman,' they said, 'what do you want?'

'I am looking for the Christ Child,' Befana replied. 'Can you tell me which way to go?'

And then the shepherds told her of a miracle.

'Last night, while we were sleeping beside our flock in this peaceful valley, all at once the dogs barked and the sheep began to bleat. Angels were singing, and a radiant star shone in the sky in a blaze of light.

'The light of the star shone upon a cave in the side of the hill. A man was guarding the entrance. An ox and a donkey lay on the straw. The Virgin Mary was kneeling beside the manger, and there lay the Christ Child, fast asleep.'

Reverently the shepherds bowed their heads. 'We fell upon our knees and gazed in wonder at the child.'

Befana was filled with joy. At last she was nearing the end of her journey. Picking up her bag of toys, she thanked the shepherds and said goodby. Then she ran across the fields until she came to the hill.

Poor Befana! The cave was dark. No one was there.

So Befana went on with her journey. For years and years she travelled on all the roads of the world, but she never caught up with the star. She never found the Christ Child.

Although Befana was terribly disappointed, she never stopped looking. She went from church to church, hoping to find the baby Jesus asleep in the Nativity at the altar. But every time she ran up to the *presepio*, she saw that the figures were not real. Even the angels hanging overhead were made of plaster.

One day Befana came to a village that was only a crossing in the road. The church was the smallest she had ever seen. But the sun was so hot that she went inside to rest.

And there in the cool darkness, with the candles burning and the sweet smell of incense in the air, she heard a voice from the stillness, echoing in the silent church.

'Poor old Befana! You have tried for so long to find the Christ Child, but the Baby Jesus is no longer in Bethlehem. His spirit rests in every child. He lives in all of them. Your place is among the children of the world.'

The voice stopped speaking. Befana sat in the darkness, her heart beating with joy, for she knew there would *always* be children waiting for her.

From that time on, Befana travelled everywhere at Christmastime to see the children, from the Alps to Sicily. Her bag was never empty. Wherever she went, she left toys for all the boys and girls, creeping into their bedrooms when they were fast asleep. But if they had been naughty, she left only a lump of coal.

The Christ Child was born a very long time ago, but Befana is still making her journey. She has left gifts for children all over the world, for the sons and daughters of kings in rich palaces and the children of poor men in shabby huts. The poorer the family, the more presents Befana wants to give, because she does not like to see anyone unhappy, especially at Christmastime.

Her greatest wish is to bring joy and gladness to the hearts of children everywhere.

Some children try to stay awake to watch Befana come and go. But it does no good, for her magic power makes her invisible.

You may hear the thump of her bag of toys upon the floor, but you will not catch a glimpse of the Christmas Witch.

And no matter how quickly you run to the door, you will see nothing but footprints in moonlit snow.